W9-AZT-973

Arty the Part-Time Astronaut

Copyright © 2000 by 3 Pounds Press. All rights reserved.

3 Pounds Press
PMB #329
25125 Santa Clara Street
Hayward, CA 94544-2109

ISBN 0-9675299-0-5

Multimedia Director: Eddie Carbin
Art Director: Greg Savoia
Author: Eddie Carbin
Illustrators: Eddie Carbin, Ron Peters, and Greg Savoia
Programmer: Eddie Carbin
Editor: Zipporah W. Collins
Production Manager: Monica Wibbelmann

www.artyastro.com

Printed in the USA

In loving memory of
Juanita Bowen Jenkins

One night Arty's parents let him camp out in the woods behind his house with his telescope, so he could do some stargazing. They outfitted him with a sleeping bag, a flashlight, and some late-night snacks. The night was so clear that Arty thought he might even be able to see Jupiter!

When Arty looked up, he saw something whoosh through the night sky right toward him.

Was that a falling star? Arty wondered.

Telescope
A device used by astronomers to help us see things far away that are too small for our eyes to see by themselves, like eyeglasses but much more powerful.

Falling star (meteor)
An object made up of rocks and ice speeding through space. As falling stars, or meteors, enter Earth's atmosphere, the surrounding air rubs against them, creating so much heat that they break into pieces. Most meteors dissolve before they make it to Earth's surface, but on occasion pieces do land.

"Wow! I need to get a closer look," Arty said, and he scrambled over rocks and tree stumps in his hurry to reach the place where the falling star had landed.

A bright glow shone from a big crater made by the impact of the meteorite. As Arty got very close, he noticed that it wasn't a meteorite at all. It was a spaceship of some sort.

Suddenly, a door opened and a little green guy crawled out.

Crater
A hole created on the surface of a planet or moon when an object hits it.

Meteorite
A piece of a meteor that doesn't dissolve in Earth's atmosphere and actually lands on Earth.

"Greetings! I'm Guplo from the planet Krandu," the little guy said.

"Hi! I'm Arty from down the street," said Arty.

"Well, isn't this a mess!" Guplo sighed. "This ship sure isn't going to fly again. My family and I were traveling through your solar system on our vacation. There I was, space-surfing behind my family's space utility vehicle, having a good old time, and kablooey! The rope broke! I went hurling into space and landed here. Now I'm going to need a new ship so I can find my family, or I may never get home. Do you happen to know where I could find a spaceship on your planet?"

"I know where to find a spaceship!" Arty exclaimed eagerly. He grabbed his bag of snacks in one hand and Guplo's hand in the other. "Let's go."

BURGER PLANET

DRIVE THRU

Off they went to the Planet Burger fun center. There, in front of the building, was a coin-operated "spaceship," the Orbiter 2000.

Arty looked doubtfully at Guplo and said, "How are we going to make this work? I only have two dimes."

"Don't worry," Guplo answered. "Just jump in and hold on. I'll handle the rest."

Arty climbed aboard, and Guplo asked, "Ready to boldly go where no kid has gone before?" Arty nodded eagerly. Guplo closed his eyes and made a strange noise. The rocket started to glow and rock back and forth. Guplo yelled, "Engage!"

With a shake, rattle, and roll of the ship, they blasted off into the sky.

Arty peered out of the window. "Look, there's my house. Cool! Light speed ahead!"

Light speed
The speed at which light can travel through empty space, which is 186,281 miles per second (299,792 km per second).

Except for the bright pinpoints of lights from the stars, the sky was black. Guplo and Arty orbited Earth and flew past the space shuttle Columbia and the Hubble telescope.

The planet in our solar system that is third closest to the sun is our home, Earth. It is special in two ways: it's the only planet in our system where water exists in liquid form and the only one known to support life. Water covers most of Earth, taking many forms, such as clouds and ice. Earth is also an active planet, because its surface is constantly changing from winds, water, earthquakes, volcanoes, and even the action of its moon.

Moons: 1
Length of day: 24 hours
Length of year: 365 days
Width across (diameter): 7,926 miles (12,756 km)

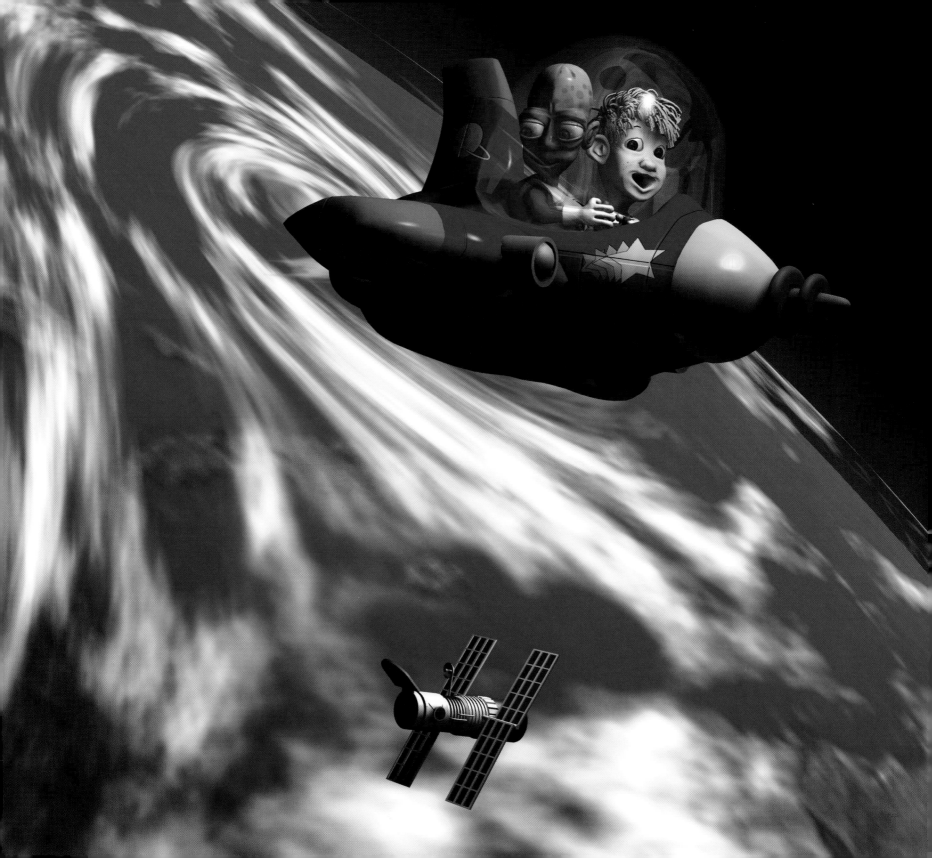

The two space travelers started their search for Guplo's family at the Moon.

"The Moon is the only place where any human has stepped, outside of Earth," Guplo noted.

Arty looked down. "Wow, look! There's the Lunar Rover that was left behind when the astronauts were here."

But Guplo saw no sign of his family's spacewagon on the Moon.

Lunar Rover
The car that the astronauts used to travel around on the surface of the Moon.

Astronaut
A person who travels in space.

The Moon orbits our planet. It is one-fourth the size of Earth and is about as wide as the United States of America. We can see the Moon in our night sky because light from the sun bounces off the surface of the Moon toward us. The Moon has a crater formation that dates back to its beginning. Scientists think that the Moon was the result of a collision between Earth and an object the size of the planet Mars about 4 billion years ago. The material from the collision went into space and formed the Moon with help from gravity.

Width across (diameter): 2,160 miles (3,476 km)
Length of orbit around the Earth: 27.5 days
Distance from Earth: 239,000 miles (384,600 km)

Next they traveled to the Sun, the star closest to Earth. Arty wiped his forehead and said, "Well, your family won't be here. It's too hot for anyone to stay here for very long."

"Yeah, they would need a tub of sunscreen!" Guplo smiled at Arty.

Our Sun is an average-size star. It's a giant ball of gas; in fact, it's so big that pressure and gravity cause the gas molecules to rub together and heat up. The Sun is the power source for our solar system, providing all the heat and light. It takes eight minutes for the light created by the sun to travel to Earth. As the biggest body in our solar system, the Sun makes up 98 percent of the stuff in the system. Its gravity holds the planets in their orbits, keeping the solar system together.

Width across (diameter): 870,000 miles (1.4 million km)
Temperature at the surface: 11,000 degrees F (6,093 degrees C)
Temperature at the center: 2.7 million degrees F (1.5 million degrees C)

Guplo's family was nowhere to be seen on the Sun, so the two voyagers made the short trip to the closest planet, Mercury.

"A year on this planet is 88 Earth days long, so your birthday would come every 88 days," Arty told Guplo.

Guplo quickly did the math. "If you're 10 years old, you would be 41 years old on this planet!"

Arty said, "Wow, that would make me older than my dad, if I lived here!"

Mercury is the planet closest to the Sun. It has a cratered surface, due to years of meteor impacts. The temperature difference on Mercury is the most extreme in the solar system. The side facing the Sun can reach more than 800 degrees F (430 degrees C), hot enough to melt most metals. The dark side, facing away from the Sun, can drop as low as -300 degrees F (-184 degrees C), cold enough to make Popsicles in seconds.

Moons: 0
Length of day: 58 Earth days
Length of year: 88 Earth days
Width across (diameter): 3,032 miles (4,878 km)

The search continued on Venus, where Arty and Guplo flew by one of the planet's active volcanoes.

"My family has a vacation house on a planet similar to this," said Guplo.

"This doesn't look like a very nice place to vacation. The temperatures here reach up to 900 degrees F," Arty replied. "It would really need a water slide. I thought 100-degree days on Earth were hot!"

Venus is the planet second from the Sun. It has a carbon dioxide atmosphere so thick that walking on its surface would feel like walking under water. Venus is the hottest of the planets, with temperatures above 900 degrees F (482 degrees C). The high temperatures are caused by the thick atmosphere's greenhouse effect. The greenhouse effect is the heat generated when light enters the atmosphere and is trapped by the thick clouds so that it cannot escape. Venus is also the only planet other than Earth known to have active volcanoes.

Moons: 0
Length of day: 243 Earth days
Length of year: 225 Earth days
Width across (diameter): 7,519 miles (12,100 km)

The next place the space travelers checked was Mars, the red planet.

"This is most likely the next place a human will land and maybe even live in the future," said Arty.

Guplo nodded. "One day Earth people will vacation here, but not until they've built hotels with pools and golf courses."

Mars is the planet fourth from the Sun. It has a reddish tint, which comes from the rusted iron soil on its surface. Mars has the highest peak and the deepest valleys in the solar system. The extinct volcano Olympus Mons rises 14 miles (23 km) high. That's three times higher than the tallest peak on the Earth, which is Mount Everest. Mars has water, in ice form, at its polar ice caps. Scientists believe that liquid water once existed on Mars, forming the valleys on its surface before it dried up.

Moons: 2
Length of day: 24.5 hours
Length of year: 687 Earth days
Width across (diameter): 4,194 miles (6,787 km)

Having still seen no sign of his family's space utility vehicle, Guplo suggested that they leave the inner planets and head toward the outer ones. To get to them, Arty and Guplo had to fly though the asteroid belt.

"Don't worry about the asteroids," Guplo told Arty. "I can fly this with my eyes closed!"

"I'd rather you didn't!" Arty said, gripping his seat tightly.

The asteroid belt is made up of thousands of asteroids found between Mars and Jupiter. It separates the inner planets from the outer planets. The particles in the belt range in size from small specks of dust to rocks 600 miles across. Gravity from nearby Jupiter prevents the asteroids from joining together and forming a tenth planet.

The two friends made it through the asteroid belt and arrived safely at Jupiter.

Arty thought that dodging through the obstacles in the belt was fun, so he asked, "Hey, Guplo, can I drive?"

Guplo thought for a moment and then said, "Well, have you ever been in a ship that moved at light speed?

"No. My family's car goes 65 mph," said Arty (104 km per hour).

"As fast as we're moving, I don't think that's such a good idea, Arty. I've already been in one crash tonight.

Jupiter, the largest planet in the solar system, is fifth from the Sun. The first of the gas giants, it is bigger than all the other planets in our system combined. It's called a gas giant because it's made entirely of gas. You wouldn't be able to land a spaceship on Jupiter because it has no surface. Jupiter has rings, like all of the other gas giant planets. Because Jupiter spins faster than any other planet, its days last only 10 hours. Jupiter is also known for its Great Red Spot, a huge whirlpool storm of gas. You could fit three Earth-size planets in the storm, and it has been going on for as long as we have been observing the planet.

Moons: 16
Rings: 2
Length of day: 10 hours
Length of year: 12 Earth years
Width across (diameter): 88,736 miles (142,800 km)

Guplo and Arty found no sign of Guplo's family on Jupiter, so on they sped to Saturn.

"Look at all the rings!" Arty exclaimed, pointing out the window.

"My home planet, Krandu, has rings like these around it. I'm starting to miss home, and I don't see my family's space utility vehicle on Saturn," said Guplo sadly.

Arty patted Guplo's arm. "Don't worry. We still have three planets to go. My mom packed some snacks. Do you want one of these cupcakes?"

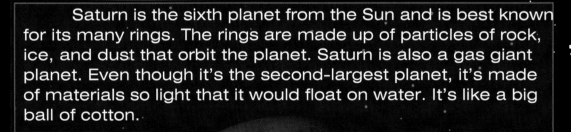

Saturn is the sixth planet from the Sun and is best known for its many rings. The rings are made up of particles of rock, ice, and dust that orbit the planet. Saturn is also a gas giant planet. Even though it's the second-largest planet, it's made of materials so light that it would float on water. It's like a big ball of cotton.

Moons: 18
Rings: Many
Length of day: 10.5 hours
Length of year: 29 Earth years
Width across (diameter): 74,500 miles (120,660 km)

Guplo's family was nowhere to be found on Saturn, so he and Arty headed for the next planet, Uranus.

"I think it's amazing how this planet seems to be lying on its side!" Arty said, looking out the window.

"I think it's amazing how they got the creamy center into these cupcakes!" said Guplo.

Uranus, the planet seventh from the Sun, is another gas giant planet. It rotates on its side, with its north pole pointing almost at the Sun. Much smaller than Saturn, Uranus has 10 thin, faint rings. It also holds the record for satellites: scientists have found 23 and are still counting.

Moons: 23
Rings: 10
Length of day: 17 hours
Length of year: 84 Earth years
Width across (diameter): 31,744 miles (51,118 km)

The next stop was Neptune.

"This is the farthest planet that our space scientists have explored with an interplanetary probe," Arty said.

"I know about those probes," said Guplo. "They send out radio signals that can travel though space for millions of miles. We've received some on Krandu."

"I once heard about a boy who could hear radio stations from the braces on his teeth. Every time he opened his mouth, his friends would hear a baseball game!" said Arty.

"I wish I could hear a radio signal from my family," replied Guplo.

Neptune is the eighth planet from the Sun and the last of the gas giant planets. It's made mostly of methane gas, which gives it a blue-green color. The winds in Neptune's atmosphere are the fastest in the solar system, traveling at speeds up to 1,243 mph (2,000 km per hour). That's almost twice the speed of sound.

Moons: 8
Rings: 4
Length of day: 19 hours
Length of year: 165 Earth years
Width across (diameter): 30,757 miles (49,528 km)

Interplanetary probe
An automated spaceship with no people aboard that is launched into space to send pictures and information about the solar system back to scientists on Earth by radio signals.

Arty and Guplo arrived at the last planet, Pluto. "Wow, look how small the Sun looks from here!" Guplo shouted.

"I'm so lucky!" said Arty. "Our astronauts go to school and train for years just to go up into space. I got to see all this in one night. I can't believe I forgot my camera!"

Pluto, the ninth planet from the Sun, was the last planet in our solar system to be discovered. Very little is known about this small planet, because it hasn't been visited by an interplanetary probe. Pluto is thought to have an icy, rocky surface with craters, like Earth's Moon, but Pluto is smaller than our Moon. It also has a moon of its own, named Charon, which is almost half the size of the planet. Pluto travels in an unusual orbit, which lets Neptune be the planet farthest from the sun during 20 years of Pluto's 248-year orbit.

Moons: 1
Length of day: 6.4 Earth days
Length of year: 248 Earth years
Width across (diameter): 1,428 miles (2,300 km)

Arty jumped out of his seat and called, "Hey, Guplo, look over there! Either I've discovered a tenth planet or that is a spaceship."

Guplo quickly turned to look out the window. "Arty, I think you've just found my family!"

"Thanks for helping me find my family's space utility vehicle, Arty," Guplo said. "I'll come back soon to learn more about your wonderful planet. But next time, it'll be a planned stop!"

"How will you let me know you're coming?" Arty asked.

"I'll keep in touch through a website on the Internet. Watch for me at www.artyastro.com."

It had been one amazing night. Arty would never see the night sky the same way again.

As he looked out the window, all Arty could think was, "No one's ever going to believe this adventure!"